YD LA MAR

SINFUL ATTRACTION

Acknowledgments

To my wonderful husband, who never bats an eye when I come up with crazy ideas, but instead just adds to it, making my stories come alive. My children, who tell me every day that they are proud of me.

To my beta readers, especially Beth. You guys are the real MVP. Thank you for always being down for whatever crazy story I throw your way with no warning. Sabrina, thank you for bouncing ideas off with me!

Mikel, my best friend. I tell you everyday how much you mean to me and my family. The badass leadership crew, you know who you are. You all inspire me everyday to level up, to try harder and to never give up.

To all my readers, thank you for giving me the chance. I hope I can continue to make you guys proud.

This little story was supposed to be in the Dark Heart anthology. Due to unforeseen circumstances, I was blessed enough to be able to bring it to you solo.

Happy reading!

Blurb

What happens when the wolf wants to eat me?

It wasn't supposed to be this way. It was supposed to be a quiet night, one like any other, while looking after Master Frank's newborn.

And then it wasn't.

A demon beast, black as death, crashed into the mansion with a vengeance, making what I thought was only a horrid legend become my reality.

Now we're captive to the most sinister, foul beast imaginable with nothing to eat. The story goes about his eyes, ears, and teeth. But it never mentioned how big his hands were, or how reverent they could be. Somehow, I have to feed this child while keeping the dark desires growing within me at bay.

My mother never told me there'd be days like this.

Courtesy Warning

Reader discretion is advised. This story may include dark themes, gore, murder, kidnapping.

It is the howl that sends chills down my spine. The rattling of the double doors steal my breath as my heart beats out of my ribs. Grabbing the baby from the crib, I back up against the wall, hiding his little face against my chest. The darkness of nightfall brought with it the drop in temperature.

My habit makes me sweat as I crouch down in the darkest corner of the mansion, praying that whatever it is outside passes over us for something else.

Tales of the beast that haunts these lands run through my mind as I silently rock the baby in my arms, trying to keep him in his slumber.

"Grab the pitchforks!"

"It's trying to get inside!"

"What would you have us do, Master Frank?" the servants scream out as more howls pierce the air.

"Get the stable boy. Saddle the horses and ready the carriage. Find the Lady and make sure the family is re—"

"Ahhh!"

The crash of wood makes me scream with the men. I

quickly cover my mouth as my ears strain to listen to what's happening.

The sound of growls, crunches, and snarls make the hair on the back of my neck stand on end as my eyes frantically look around for an exit. The windows are large and closed shut, the locks hard to maneuver with a baby in my arms.

A crash against the baby's bedroom door and a snarl makes me jump in fright. My body is sweating from my fear of being trapped here with the little one. Suddenly, a claw splinters the wood. It's dark, sharp, and coated with blood.

I no longer hear the sound of the men outside. Not a word or a moan of pain.

I clutch my rosary and pray for the Lord to look over both of us as the beast slams its body again and again against the door, breaking it off its hinges, sending pieces of wood flying against the baby's furniture.

"I will protect you with my life, baby Adam," I whisper against his soft, peach fuzz hair right before I start to say the Lord's prayer.

The shadow looms over us both, bringing with it the scent of death and blood right before I close my eyes and hug baby Adam close to my bosom.

One

SISTER JEANNA

My bones feel stiff from the cold that seeps into my body from below. Groaning, I shift my weight by pushing myself up. My head pounds. Rubbing my temples, the bandeau and veil shifts and I'm reminded of what happened before I passed out.

The baby.

"Where are you? Where am I?" I open my eyes to find cavernous rocks around me, the sound of water trickling nearby echoes and distracts me as I climb to my feet, dust my habit skirt off, and begin searching around the vicinity for baby Adam.

My hands run across the cold cavern walls, my palms clammy from nervousness. The edges are jagged, sometimes cutting my skin, sending spikes of pain like a papercut through me. I don't know how I got here and I'm more afraid of the fact that I don't remember anything beyond holding the child while the beast...

My fear increases exponentially the longer I search with no success. From shadow to shadow, my eyes scan my surroundings only finding remnants of what could have lived here. Scattered bones of small creatures, appear every now and again as if the resident had purposely scattered the carcasses to reduce clues.

"Adam?" My low toned whisper sounds loud around my ears.

The cavern is cold and dank, the temperature never varying much no matter if I travel through tunnels or reach another open area. There is a subtle glow of light that filters in occasionally from cracks in the ceiling as I go from cavern room to cavern room.

A small hiccup wafts through the air from my left and I pick up my skirt and run, the rosaries on my hip rattle and expose my position. My heart beats erratically, the hope overflowing in my chest. I reach a warmer room at the mouth of this neverending cave system, skid, and fall to my knees when I see baby Adam in a pile of leaves and moss, still swaddled. His little hands are poking out, waving around, looking for comfort.

I choke and the baby cries. Gently leaning in to grab him, I bring him close to me to combine our warmth. He roots against my chest and I cry, the tears falling on his precious little face.

I didn't think he would survive. I didn't—

A growl reverberates through the cave and my head snaps up to find a beast as black as night standing on two legs. Fog escapes his mouth and nostrils as he heaves in breaths. Covered in dark fur, his eyes are as cool and intense as the oceans that surround us on this island—if we're still here.

The bundle in my arms wriggles and my fight or flight response kicks in. Slowly standing, I keep my body slightly crouched and unthreatening, covering the baby's face in my chest. The heavy wet muslin crackles and makes noises as the baby struggles to understand why we are in this position.

The beast's lips curl into a snarl. The cresting of the sun's rays come up behind him, cloaking his face in shadows with hues of oranges and violets. The contrast in the moment is jarring. The beast's ivory colored fangs extrude beyond his lips, the saliva stringing as he snaps his jaws in front of me, aggravated.

I say a silent prayer in my mind. "J-just let us leave. We mean you no harm. He's just a baby. I need to take care of him. Please," I try.

He snarls and snaps his jaw again, sending me to the ground on my behind in surprise. My body shakes but my mind remains strong. Old instincts threaten to reveal themselves as my eyes sharpen, judging the distance and time it would take to try and dodge him in my attempt to escape this cave with this much fabric holding me back. The Lord did not put me in this child's life without reason. He needs me. Now more than ever.

We'll take our chances out there. We'll be okay.

As if knowing my thoughts, the beast lands on all four and prowls towards me. Scooting back until I hit a wall, I look around me to see if I can use anything as a weapon of opportunity. Nothing but pebbles and small animal bones lay beside me, not big enough to cause damage or distraction. I refuse to use my wooden cross as a weapon.

"You're pathetic, girl. Just like your whore of a mother!" Spittle flies out his mouth and lands on my face as the tears continue to flow.

My mother lies on the ground, unconscious. I try to rouse her, shake her, whisper her name but the only thing that changes is the blooming of the bruise left on her face under the welt left by his ring.

"Momma! Wake up! Please! He's coming again!"

Right as my father takes a few steps toward me with menace in his smile, my mother launches herself and tackles him to the ground, knocking his head against the corner of the side table. He's stunned enough to not move. Momma grabs my hand and runs with us out the door and doesn't stop until she's able to seek sanctuary in St. Mary's of Misty Isles.

Standing up, I keep my back against the wall, watching the beast's every move.

I can't let my mother's efforts in saving us go to waste. I had a difficult time adjusting to the ways of the convent, not perfect by any means, but it led me to baby Adam. I became saved to become a savior to this poor child—something I wished someone did for me and my mother.

The beast swipes his claws and I dodge, his nails slicing through my dress. *Lord, forgive me for what I must do.* Jostling Adam in my arm, I rip off the coif from my head and wind it in my fist. It's the only thing I can think of.

The beast prowls, his hackles rising as he stares at what's in my hand.

When he lunges, I swing it down and slap him on the nose with the starched white fabric, the soft black muslin providing me enough flexibility to utilize it like a whip. He yelps and I run. The uneven terrain of the cave's floor makes it hard for me to get a good footing, the fabric of my habit catching under my feet. It doesn't help that the entrance of the cave has a slight incline, either.

I slip and land on my knee with a hard crash. Hissing, I push myself up to standing and begin moving again.

The sun's rays warm my face as hope explodes and then, just as quickly, extinguish when the beast pounces on me, slamming my shoulder into the ground.

I cry out in pain as I force myself to roll just enough to protect the baby's head with my hand. *We were so close!*

Flashes of my father taking my mother down, hammer inside of my head—memories I thought long forgotten resurfaces with a vengeance.

My legs kick, landing on flesh and sometimes missing the

target. *I can't give up, not now!* The ripped skirt helps me to make a wide arch with my leg as I slam it into the beast's face, knocking him enough to the side for me to slip from his grasp.

Crawling on hands and knees, I make it to the ledge only to have the beast grab my leg. My hands claw at the ground furiously, my nails breaking off as he pulls me back even harder. The blood that coats my fingertips makes my hand slip and lose grip as my screams echo into the daybreak.

Two

HEMMING

I tried to tell her of what lurks out beyond the cave. She wouldn't listen. Instead, she smelled of fear and my own concern for the pup grew. Does she not realize the danger she puts them in by traveling alone on this island? Every corner lurks a monster and not all of them are covered in fur such as I, the last son of the Murk clan on this forsaken island.

She scratches and claws at my face like the fierce female she is, aggravating me and impressing me all at once. The rage that consumed me during my hunt of the humans in their opulent home died down the moment I saw the woman and the cub. What kind of monster leaves the most vulnerable to fend for themselves?

"Cease this at once! You do not understand the dangers that lurk out there! You must remain in the den!"

She doesn't understand me. Her eyes widen with fear and determination right before she tries to kick me again, but this time I'm able to anticipate the move and dodge it.

The smell of fresh blood stings my nostrils as I pull her and the cub under me, covering her with the entirety of my body to calm her fears.

She shakes, holding the cub closer to her chest the way she always does—the way it caught my eye the first time.

"I tire of battles, little one. I do not wish to fight anymore. Just stay in the den where it is safe, I beg of you," I whisper against her.

I know my appearance can be off putting. The pack has taught me this time and time again. She tenses up and I sigh, frustrated that we cannot communicate effectively for this all to run smoothly.

"Do you have another male you need to return to?" She doesn't answer, of course.

What if she did? The hairs on my back bristle at the thought. "If that is the case, why has he not protected you like he should?! What worthy male would leave his female and cub alone to beasts?"

Like fallen prey, the female tries to keep herself as still and small as possible, her bloody fingers covering the pup's head for protection.

I whine at her injuries, upset that it had to come to this. If she does have a male elsewhere, her devotion leaves me in envy.

Licking her wounds, she hisses and pulls back, mumbling something I cannot comprehend. I try to stare at her lips but she hides those as well. Growling, I earnestly lick all her wounds, letting her know that I am more than capable of caring for her. No male has ventured to my home since I brought them here. No male worthy of such a proud and brave female such as she.

She lets out a small sound and my tongue stops midway on her fingers. Breathing slowly, I remain still, waiting for her next move.

She lifts her head from the pup's and stares at me with curiosity and caution.

Pulling my tongue back, I climb off her and nudge her to stand. She says something but her tone lacks anger, so I try again.

She moves at my command and my tail wags. I watch as she slowly makes her way deeper inside the den. Following her on all fours, I bring myself to stand on two legs and point to the nest for her and the pup to rest in.

Her eyes sparkle with understanding as her brow pinches in confusion. Having been around humans enough, I can decipher some of their expressions better than my brethren.

She sits on her rear and cradles the pup who is crying in hunger.

"Comfort the pup. I shall return with food for you both."

She stares at me and I shake my body in disappointment once again. Turning, I trudge towards the entrance on all fours, looking over my shoulder right before I leave.

She continues to stare while rocking the babe. I do not think she will be foolish enough to try and leave again, not with him making so much noise.

Deciding that it will have to do for now, I leap over the ledge and sprint through the woods that camouflage my home. Leaping against boulders and digging my paws into the fresh earth, my wet nose strains to catch any scent of prey nearby.

There.

The rabbit dashes away, crunching on the leaves. My ears swivel as my paws follow its lead. My heart races with excitement and my mouth salivates. He jumps and dodges sharply to the left under a fallen log. I snarl, leaping over it and cutting him off with my landing. He doesn't skid to a stop in time and I open my maws for a fatal bite. The rabbit cries like a pup and my mind is redirected back to the den.

Judging by the size of the rabbit, it will be enough to sustain us for another few days.

Jogging back toward home, my ears swivel when I hear the sound of men speaking in whispers. The hair on the back of my neck stands on end as I pick up my pace and hide among the shadow of the trees during my travels back.

Swoosh. Thunk!

An arrow lodges right beside me, sending my body into high gear. I leap and run between the trees, leading the hunters in circles until I hear their voices raise in panic at losing their target. Crawling into a small tunnel, I claw my way until it reaches a higher ceiling. Shaking off the dirt that's collected on my fur, I stretch and straighten on all fours, my nails clicking on the solid rock ground down the back path toward the den.

The female speaks and my body tenses. Who is she speaking to? Slinking through the tunnels, I quickly find myself back at the den only to see her staring down at the pup in her arms. His small cries turn into whimpers and he continuously tries to root against her chest.

He's hungry.

Purpose fuels my next movements as I make myself known, dropping the kill beside them. The female shrieks and scuttles away. I crouch on two legs, grabbing the rabbit with my claws, hoping to emulate human males in a sign of offering.

Handing it to her, she shakes her head vehemently and I snarl at the frustration of trying to understand her. Why must she be so difficult? The pup is hungry and she probably is too.

"It is for you. You must feed. The pup hungers in his wails, do you not hear it?"

I bring it to my mouth and emulate eating and she sharpens her gaze on me then to the rabbit in my hand.

She says something and I sit on my hind legs, tilting my head trying to understand it.

Three

JEANNA

Did he bring this to feed us?

"I can't eat it like that. The baby cannot eat it."

He tilts his head and I become ever more frustrated. I was afraid of him hunting us if I tried to escape again. My nail beds throb from my injury as I continue to rock a crying baby Adam. He's hungry. The wolf-beast knows this too. It must be why he went to bring us meat.

If we are to try and get along while we're here, we're going to have to establish some form of communication somehow.

My stomach rumbles at that very moment and the beast's tail wags. It would be endearing if it wasn't for how frightfully large and dark he is. The sunlight glints against his eyes, sending small spikes of fear through me.

How do I know he's not fattening us up for other nefarious reasons? The sisters would have chastised me for that line of thinking. I need to give him the benefit of the doubt, but the ugliness of my past tells me otherwise.

"I-I need it cooked, please."

He lowers himself to all four and hands me the dead rabbit, cautiously. Baby Adam wails with all this jostling and my heart constricts at his suffering. It isn't the babe's fault we are in this situation. He never asked to be brought into this world.

I do the only thing I know to do to pacify him for the time being. Turning my back to the beast, I undo the top of my habit dress and slip my right breast out, letting baby Adam suckle. He quiets immediately.

The beast looks around my shoulder and I slap his face accidentally with the back of my hand when I try to shoo him away.

He grumbles and sneaks back again but lower to the ground. I can see his black wet nose flaring the closer he gets. Turning away from him again, he grumbles some more.

"If you aren't busy, I suggest you go out and find something to make a fire so we can cook this food. Something along the lines of branches and wood."

I hear the sound of a huff, then his nails along the solid rocky ground of the cave and, suddenly, he disappears out the entrance.

Did he understand me? The baby bites my nipple and I yelp, my attention pulled back to him. He struggles and bats at my flesh, finally crying from frustration once more against my breast.

The sound of wood crashing behind me makes me jump, only further agitating the baby.

Branches scatter on the ground. The wolf reemerges with more held in his arms as he drops them at his feet. Getting on all fours, he pushes them all into a large pile and wags his tail, sitting back on his haunches.

"What do you want me to do with that? I have the baby in my arms," I tell him

He tilts his head and I stifle a laugh. The baby bats against my chest and I sigh, trying to get him to suckle again. I don't have anything else to offer him but I've accompanied Sister Elizabeth enough with midwifery to understand what the baby needs. The skin to skin contact should also calm him.

Adam makes frustrated noises against me as I stand and look around for loose stones I may be able to strike together for firestarting.

Memories of my mother and I trying to leave my father float to the forefront of my mind.

"It's going to get cold soon. Gather some wood."

I do as my mother asks and put them all in a pile. She pulls a couple of rocks from the pocket of her apron and places them beside her foot.

"Let's see if we can do it with the branches alone. If not, the stones should be a good backup. Always remember this. This might not be the last time we have to stay out here."

"Yes, Mama."

We stayed out in the woods for the entire night, my mother teaching me how to start a fire with the stones.

My father found us in the morning, beating my mother and dragging us both back home by the hair.

My eyes prick with tears, blurring my vision as I balance baby Adam while leaning down to grab a sizable stone.

I can feel his hot breaths against my neck before I see him. Startling, I turn so fast I drop the baby. His large claws catch him mid air and bring Adam to his chest. The baby's little fists clench around the beast's chest hair, pulling in irritation as he wails once more.

The beast growls, making my heart jump. I'm about to throw the stone at his face when he bends his head down and nuzzles the baby, making his cries turn into giggles.

Lord forgive me for my judgment.

I make sure to concentrate on every sound and expression coming from the baby as I continue to wander around looking for another stone. When I find one, I sigh in relief and walk back toward the pile of branches. The baby coos and giggles, letting my mind rest easy.

Sitting down, I strike them together with no success despite the sparks that fly out. Maybe it needs some sort of kindling to catch. There's nothing around me that will work—nothing except possibly my ripped up habit cloth made from cotton.

Placing the stones on the ground beside me, I try to rip the bottom hem only successfully making my fingers throb from the pain of having lost my fingernails earlier. I bite my bottom lip and try again. Tears track down my cheeks but I close my eyes and—

A warm palm stops my movements. I look up to find the beast crouching beside me with Adam cradled against his chest. He grumbles, the flesh of his lips moving against his fangs. I wonder if he's talking to me? Telling me what a fool I am for thinking that two stones would do anything other than make noise when striking against one another.

"It does seem silly, doesn't it? Who in their right mind might even think of this to begin with?"

He tilts his head and doesn't respond.

"We take for granted everything we have at our disposal." I huff out a humorless laugh, my eyes tearing up once more. "But when it comes down to survival, would Adam and I even make it out there alone?"

Knowing he can't understand me gives me the courage to voice my fears aloud.

He drops his hand and his sharp claws inadvertently rip the hem of my robe. I choke out a laugh at the coincidence and bring the fabric up to my face. Maybe I can use my teeth?

Sticking it in my mouth, I bite down and pull.

Four

HEMMING

Does she not eat meat? Have I been mistaken? I recognized her tongue forming the sound that indicates wood. I've heard many of the human males talk about this in the forest that surrounds us while they are out on a hunt. They gather them in piles.

I continue to coo at the pup as I watch her tear the bottom of her coverings—or attempt to. She struggles since the loss of her nails and guilt assaults me.

Leaning in, I pat the pup on the back and hand it to her. She looks at me curiously but takes the babe. Extending my own claws, I tear the bottom of her covering quickly. She yelps and my eyes snap to hers, worried, I hurt her in the process. I don't think I did.

Tilting my head, I hand her the ripped piece, wondering what she wants with it. I watch as she cautiously takes it from my hand and bunches it up against the pile of wood. The pads of her fingers are soft against my calloused hands.

Bristling my back, I shake my head and concentrate on what she's doing.

She wishes to cook them? I've never seen it done but I also do not know enough about human customs to understand all of their ways.

She strikes the rocks again and one of the sparks catches the fabric, quickly burning. I lunge and grab her, pulling away from the danger. She shakes a little in my arms as I look over my shoulder at the wood that catches fire. What is this fascination humans have with fire and flame? The smell of embers can always be caught in the wind on a downdraft when one is next to any type of human encampment.

The female speaks rapidly and sounds in distress. My instincts kick in and I lick her face trying to calm her nerves. She bats me away but I continue to lick her hand and her injury, a whine escaping because of my guilt.

She sighs and pats my face before rocking the baby who seems to be lost in the sight of my tongue lolling out the side.

He tries to bat at it and I lick his face making him giggle and scrunch his little nose.

The female shoves the babe into my arms and crawls around me back to the pile of wood, striking her stones.

My eyes swivel with caution as I watch the sparks fly again. My tail wraps around me and touches her backside for my own peace of mind.

There is smoke growing and suddenly, she bends to blow at it. This doesn't make any sense. Why strike for embers if she is only going to blow it out? Maybe she is mad, not fully in her right mind. This would make a lot of sense, really.

When a flame grows, my tail wraps around her ankle, readying itself to pull her out of the way if necessary.

She jumps with elation and I yelp in surprise, protecting the pup's head from her movements. I yelp and bark at her to calm herself. She turns and her face is full of teeth. My ears flatten, unsure how to interpret this—is it a threat or something else?

She points at the fire and then the rabbit, simulating eating with her hands and my ears straighten and stand.

She wants me to burn the rabbit? Standing up on my hind legs, I carry the pup into the nest, pushing the moss and leaves around to create a higher wall around him. Grabbing the rabbit, I tentatively attempt to toss it into the flame.

"NO!"

My arm stops mid movement. I've heard this word before. Seen human females cry in distress when males force them to be mounted. My ears flatten in confusion at her chastisement. I have done no such thing to her. Why would she scold me so?

She mumbles something else quickly, straightening her arms with her palms facing me. I stare at her declawed fingers and sink even lower, tucking my tail with the weight of everything I've caused her. This is why she chastises me. I deserve every bit of it. Dropping the rabbit on the ground, I crawl to her and whine. Nudging my nose against her palm, I lick it in earnest to show her how sorry I am. Do humans grow claws again once they've lost them? My ears are so flat against my head they ache.

She huffs and falls to her knees as the pup coos in the nest. Turning her palm up, I stick my head there and rest it in submission. I need her forgiveness. How are we to den together if she ends up hating me? How did my sire and dam do it? It seemed easy through the eyes of a pup. Then again, neither of them was human...

"What can I do, female, to earn your forgiveness? We were both running on high emotions and now I face the consequences of my actions boldly. What would you task me to do? I can find you a million rabbits and branches if that is what you wished of me."

She tilts her head, the cloth that covers her, gaping at the front, revealing pale flesh underneath. She pats my head and my tail unravels from beneath me. This is good, yes? I've said something good? She wishes for me to hunt?

She sighs before picking up the rabbit in her hands and pulling at its fur. I blink and stare at her ministrations, wondering if she wanted me to cut it open for her since she does not have any claws.

You fool. Of course, she does. You just said it! She has no claws!

Grumbling at myself, I snarl at my stupidity. She gasps and I put my palm out the way she did. She calms as I slowly reach for the rabbit. She hands it over without argument, watching me closely with cautious eyes. Using one claw, I rip it down the middle and hand it back to her. Her eyes sparkle as she flaps her own around to try and communicate something with me.

I-I think she wants me to skin it. Simple enough. With my claws and maw, I rip the rabbit's skin off with ease, handing her the delicate meat and muscle inside.

She bares her teeth again but I can sense her elation. This is good, then. This is what she wanted. She scrambles and looks around her with her brows pinched. Suddenly, she reaches into the pile of wood still in flames and I bark, making her jump. She rattles off something and I whine as she pulls off the sticks that haven't burned yet.

She takes the meat from my hand and spears it. That's interesting. The pup has crawled out of the nest and I scoop him up before he reaches the flame. I turn to find the female turning the meat over the fire, the meat sizzling and scenting of something I've come to connect with human villages.

So this is what they do. They sear their meat over flame. My tail wags as the pup pulls at my chest hair trying to shove it in his mouth.

"In a little bit, you will have your food. Your mother is doing what she must so you must be patient there, pup."

The baby laughs when I nudge my wet nose against his cheek. He is a squirmy little fellow. I place him on the ground and he rolls.

Once the food is deemed edible, the female blows on it as she brings it over to show me. I huff at her little skewer. My mouth waters at the sight of her peeling off a piece of the meat and putting it into her mouth. I wonder how it tastes.

She must read my mind because she rips off another piece and offers it to me. My ears swivel and my tail wags before I gently take it with my mouth. The flavors burst on my tongue and my tail wags harder, slapping the pup as he tries to catch it.

"Oh!" she exclaims, handing me the skewer and picking the babe up.

She bares her teeth again and rocks him. He smiles back before he tries to root against her chest. He hungers. Ripping off meat as best as I can, I hand it to him. The female shakes her head.

"No..." She says something afterward that I cannot understand. Why can't he eat it? Pups eat everything.

"He is hungry, female. Would you have him starve? There is enough for both of you. I can always hunt again."

She tilts her head and pulls out her breast, shoving it into the pup's mouth. Ah, so he has not weaned just yet.

The babe suckles and pulls at her teat. With the rabbit in hand, I begin peeling the meat off and feeding her.

She looks at me strangely before taking the first bite. I continue until almost all of the rabbit is gone. A mother needs nourishment to make milk.

The baby whines and wails with his little paws, hitting her flesh and I chastise him, snapping my jaws.

The female pulls him away and I bring both of my claws up, palm facing out. Her tense body calms and I let out a sigh. This is going to be difficult.

Five

JEANNA

I must have been more tired than I thought. After eating rabbit, my eyes begin to get heavy. Crawling back into the nest, I lie on my side, letting baby Adam suckle. Switching breasts, I let him fight until he tires himself out, falling asleep, drooling against me.

The days go by and the beast and I develop a sort of routine. He took us out to a river to wash up and drink fresh water, something I was quite grateful for because we were both starting to smell a bit ripe.

At first, I couldn't bring myself to disrobe in front of him. He was, after all, a male. But soon enough, even my own smell was affecting me. I washed my habit and did my best to wring it and dry it out in the sun before we returned to the den.

The beast had caught us many things but my favorite was quail. Plucking its feathers was a chore but the end result was so worth it. My nails haven't grown back yet but the nail beds have fully healed. One strange day, the beast came home with a few bowls and utensils. I questioned him but he said nothing, only shoving the items at me with his tail wagging. I accepted his gift with humility. Who am I to question how he chooses to take care of our needs? It's not like I ever attempted to go find anything of the sort. His dark eyes sharpened and sparkled the moment I took the items from his hands. I filed the observation away in the back of my mind.

Each day, I tried my best to introduce baby Adam to solid food, but it was difficult. He only accepted very little after I chewed it for him. It was a start, if anything. He was beginning to lose weight and it worried me daily.

I also began to wonder how I would be able to communicate with the beast. I wanted to tell him that we may need to capture a female goat if baby Adam continues to refuse eating solids.

Today, I'm sitting in the den with the babe at my breast once more while I chew on some meat I dried a few days past. The beast walks around the den, adding more things to the nest to build it up. With three bodies, the space is beginning to get tight or perhaps it is all in my mind.

I was uncomfortable at first but when the cold of the night seeped into my bones, I was more than happy to share his body heat. He eventually became used to wrapping his dark furred arm around us and pulling us closer into the warmth he provided.

My face still flushes at the thought. It's so inappropriate but we need to survive. It's not like anything has happened between us besides nightly embraces.

Swallowing the hard textured meat, a strange shudder runs through me and, suddenly, I can feel my breast get heavy with ache. I moan aloud as the baby chokes on the milk that spills out of me and into his mouth. His face is coated with the liquid as his mouth tries to latch on to my breast desperately to drink what my body finally offers.

The ache slowly subsides the more he suckles and empties them.

I never knew I could do this. I was only trying to pacify him while I tried to give him solids for nutrition. I cry as I pray thanks to the Lord for blessing me with food for Adam. He's going to make it. We're going to make it.

The beast gets up on all fours from relaxing nearby and walks toward me. My face feels warm and flush from the baby emptying one breast and quickly latching on to the other like he is starved—and he is.

A wet nose touches my empty breast and nipple and I gasp from the sensitivity. He sniffs and nuzzles my skin, furthering my embarrassment. I try to push him away but he pushes back and licks the droplets of milk that leaks out, whining.

"Stop. You're not supposed to do that," I say breathlessly. This feels so wrong... but nothing about what's happened in our lives thus far has been right.

My entire life turned upside down that fateful night. Surviving has been my number one concentration. Why haven't I tried to escape once the beast let his guard down? Why have I become so used to his presence and the life we've created together with baby Adam?

On the inside, I know the truth. It's my fear of having my relationship with them torn apart once I make it back to society. What would happen to baby Adam? Would he be passed back and forth to strangers in a system that wouldn't take his interest to heart? What kind of existence would that be? What was the actual reason why the beast attacked Master Frank's home to begin with?

I look into the beast's eyes and timidly cast my gaze down. We've become a sort of unit, him and I and the child. Life is so simple and peaceful. Would it be so wrong to want to stay here and just be that? A family? Returning would cause more complication, heartache and trauma than I would ever want to bestow on either of them.

As for me? I've had enough trauma in my past to last three lifetimes. I would offer myself to shoulder all of theirs if I could.

The beast grumbles something and leaps out the cave entrance in a hurry. Baby Adam is beginning to go lax in my arms, drunk from the milk he's ingested. Slowly getting to my feet, I cradle the baby and gently place him in our new nest. It looks softened by more moss rather than leaves and I am thankful for it. The crackle of their dried bodies would wake Adam during a fitful slumber. Looking at him now, I highly doubt he will be moving much in his nap.

I watch as he drools to the side, a soft smile playing on my face. My breasts still feel heavy with ache and I try to caress them to relieve it but it doesn't help.

Not knowing when the beast will return, my breasts feel hard, like rocks, and my fears grow to insurmountable heights. What if there is something wrong? Am I supposed to be doing something?

The only relief that came was when baby Adam suckled and removed the milk. Frantically looking around, I grab the bowl and try to squeeze my right breast and nipple over it. Milk drips and squirts without rhyme or reason but my breasts feel a semblance of relief and tears track down my cheeks.

The rustle of bushes right outside our cave dwelling is the only warning I get before the beast reenters the den with something in his mouth, something large. His eyes look to me and then to Adam. Trudging toward me on all fours, he drops what looks like a small fox from his mouth.

"Wow. That's quite a catch, Beast."

He doesn't respond, instead choosing to stare at what my

hands are doing. Heat rushes to my face as I quickly cover myself and place the bowl down, pretending to be done. My left breast hardens to rocks as I try to bite down and hide my pain.

His nostrils flare but he says nothing, grabbing the fox, walking on all fours to a corner and beginning to gut the kill.

HEMMING

She smells different. Her milk has come in and I find myself enamored with her biology. How does a dam give birth to a pup and not have food for it? I've watched their interactions and the only conclusion my mind has given me is that one of the human males must have caused some sort of trauma to her body.

The thought angers me more than it should have. This strange female and her pup have dug themselves under my skin, fitting their little bodies inside of my heart the longer we're together.

Some nights, I wonder if it will be the one where she decides she's had enough of playing den with me and tries to escape again.

But it never happens. It never comes. My chest tightens at the thought of her not only choosing to be under my protection but wanting it as well.

I never realized how lonely my existence was until my nights were filled with their warmth.

During one of the nights while they were fast asleep, I snuck out of the nest to find locations inside the den to create ventilation holes so that the smoke from the fire may escape discreetly. More bushes had to be gathered to cover our entrance. I wanted to decrease the chances of random humans stumbling upon our home when we took our leave for the river.

Living with others has kept me busy. I enjoy it more than I thought I would.

I meticulously gut and skin the kill, making sure I take the utmost care for her nutrition. The skill of burning meat to her liking was easy to learn and I am happy to be the one to provide for her.

"Female, come. I've skewered the meat for you and the babe."

With her eyes casted down in constant submission, she tentatively grabs it from me. Why does she not look at me directly the way she usually does? Shoving my nose under her chin, I chuck it up to force her eyes on me.

She huffs and laughs under her breath. Her eyes take a peek at me from the side as she starts her fire. Licking her face quickly to tell her I'm not angry, I take the skewer from her hands and turn it over the open flame.

The meat cooks quickly, the flame consuming the melted fat, sizzling. The female removes herself from my line of sight and my ears flick back to listen.

She softly moans and my mind harbors images of what I found coming into the den today: her bent over her bowl, squeezing the milk out of her teats. I lick my lips and chastise myself for even thinking of her that way, a guest of my home.

But we have become beyond that, haven't we? The nights my arms reach for her and the pup, brings warmth to the tip of my ears.

I clear my throat as the meat begins to singe more than it should. "Female."

Though we cannot understand each other, we both have become familiar and recognize the sounds we make to address one another.

She turns and reveals a face a few shades redder than what it was earlier. My tail thumps and I force myself to keep my emotions under control. Her smell is different. It calls to an instinct buried within me.

Clearing my throat again, I call her over using my free hand. She crawls to me and my cock begins to extrude from its skin. My focus sharpens on her movements and my nostrils flare the closer she gets, taking in the scent of milk. Gnashing my teeth together, I peel the meat off the skewer and feed her.

This has also become another routine between us. Her claws have yet to grow back. The thought deflates my desire enough for me to shift my weight and face her, feeding her easier.

She sighs when she is full and I set the skewer aside on a boulder I have moved against the wall. She had expressed displeasure when I placed it on the ground. I've learned my lesson. She did not eat for two days, causing me unease and guilt.

I watch as she crawls into the nest by the pup who is rousing from his nap. The night comes upon us as I scatter the branches to help the fire die down. The flames would cause too much attention to our den despite the coldness the darkness brings.

Making sure no one is looking, my curiosity gets the better of me as I crawl on all fours towards the bowl she left behind. She thinks I do not remember, but the scent has been calling to me all night.

Creeping closer to the ground, I look over my shoulder one

more time to make sure no one is awake. Reaching the bowl, I sniff... then sniff some more. Sticking my tongue out, I lap up the sweet taste and find myself ravenous for more. When the bowl slaps against the ground with a loud noise, my hackles rise and I stare at the thing with accusation. How did it get empty so fast? Tucking my tail under me, I look over at the nest again. No one has stirred. Sheepishly leaving the evidence, I try to lick my lips to rid myself of any residue left behind.

The female and pup slumber quietly, their eyes behind their lids, flitting with whatever dreams overtake them. Shaking my fur, I stretch my body before crawling in behind her, pulling them close to me. Burying my muzzle into the crook of her neck, I breathe in deeply to memorize her scent.

The pup struggles, kicks until he dislodges himself from her arms where he turns to the side and drools. I chuff a laugh and the female turns toward my chest to snuggle into my warmth. I lick her hair, relaxing myself into a restful state. The female softly moans in distress and I push her away far enough to look at her.

Her eyes open at half mast. She bites her lip and moans again.

"What is wrong, little female? Do you hurt?"

Her eyes gleam with tears and my heart skips a beat in fear. Suddenly, her little hands cover her teats, pulling her covering down and leaking between her fingers when she squeezes them. I lick my lips, unable to stop myself.

She grimaces, exposing her little teeth and I whine. "What do you need me to do? Does it hurt here?"

My tail wags slowly, unsure of what course of action I should take—knowing what course of action I *want* to take. Her eyes shut as she squeezes the end, letting her milk flow down her wrist. Quickly shifting positions, I lick her hand in a show of support. I don't like to see her in pain. The milk is sweet like what was in the bowl and I wonder how much better it would taste warm...

Something takes over and all my focus shifts to satisfying that burning curiosity. Pushing her hand away with my nose, I lick the sickly sweet milk off her skin. Her flesh is hard, full. She needs relief and the pup is still snoring soundly beside us.

She leaks and I lick her again, eliciting a gasp and my eyes snap to hers in hunger.

Seven

JEANNA

It hurts. My breasts feel like rocks under my skin and pinching my nipples doesn't give me enough relief. Baby Adam is snoring and I feel so bad for wanting to wake him to end my misery. My breasts feel hot, almost angry. I fear that not relieving them will bring some sort of infection.

The beast licks my hand and my thoughts turn to things I should not want or crave. What would it be like for him to empty me? Would he suck harder than the baby, empty me faster? The mere thought of that makes me spasm between my legs.

I want that relief so badly that when he shoves my hand away with his cold nose, I let him. When his warm, wet tongue goes over my sensitive nipples, I bite back a moan. There's pain that mixes with pleasure.

Forgive me father for what I'm about to do.

Cradling his face, I force him tighter against me, telling him what I want with my body language all the while praying inside my mind for forgiveness. His eyes sparkle as the soft part of his lips nibble my breast while his tongue presses against it. I hiss in the most unladylike manner.

Despite my embarrassment at the situation, my pain forces me to squeeze my breast as he continues to lap and nibble, dripping some of my milk onto his tongue to entice him. He whines and I scissor my legs together. If only he could—

I'm taken by surprise when his tongue and mouth creates a suction and he begins to draw gulps and gulps of milk. I moan without meaning to, caressing his face in thanks as my body shudders with relief from the pressure underneath my skin. My right breast slowly feels less tight, the more he draws into his mouth. It almost makes me delirious with other emotions.

"I shouldn't like this. But it feels so good," I whisper. Closing my eyes, I turn from my side onto my back and pull his face with me.

He covers my body with his dark fur and feels like a warm blanket in the middle of the night. My body is sweating from my left breast leaking in sync with what he's doing to my right. The warm liquid cools as it tracks down the side of my body and onto the nest.

My hand cradles the left breast, trying to massage around it as the beast empties my right. Sighing with relief when he pulls off, I push his head against my other one and yelp when he latches on automatically.

His hips undulate against me and the ripped fabric by my leg shifts enough to feel something wet protruding against my inner thigh.

A flash of fear runs through me. Do I push him off? But my left breast still aches with heaviness and he feels so warm where he is. *This is so wrong. What is wrong with me?* Memories of my father having his way with my mother with the door open during my childhood flashes before my eyes and I twist until the beast's mouth unlatches so that I may roll over, covering my face.

It's all so wrong, everything that's happened. Why haven't I tried to return to society? The convent is probably still searching for me, right? What would they say if they found out I allowed this to happen? But nothing happened. I was in pain. The beast was trying to help. A million thoughts run through my mind and I still don't know what to think of it all.

His cold nose pushes at my shoulder, a small growl coming from his chest. Tears spring forth and I feel so lost. Have I turned away from the path I should be on? I don't even know what the right path is anymore. The beast saved us. He saved me and Adam. He feeds us, takes care of us, and gives us a home.

How can that be so wrong? The Lord teaches us love above all else. That no man should be alone. Turning to look over my shoulder, I stare into the beast's eyes. This male has been alone for who knows how long. God sent a helper to the first man, a woman. Was I placed on his path for a reason?

The beast licks my arm slowly, as if asking forgiveness, and I close my eyes. My left breast becomes heavier and hardens again. Groaning in pain, a clawed hand forces me onto my back and his mouth is on me again with vigor. He's trying to take the pain away. He's taking care of me. How can anyone blame such intentions? He draws a few mouthfuls and licks the milk that escapes his lips, leaking down my side. The heat in my breasts die down and I caress his dark furred head again in gratitude.

He huffs and I try to hide a smile. I've come to understand this to be his low chuckle.

"We are a strange pair, aren't we? The Lord teaches us that above all, we must love one another deeply. I appreciate every-thing you've done for me and baby Adam."

His eyes flick to the child at the mention of his name before flicking back. The baby continues to snore soundly in his little pocket in the nest.

The beast covers me again and I take a sharp inhale. He licks the underside of my breast and I squirm, biting my bottom lip. When his nose nuzzles the crook of my neck and licks there with tenderness, I let out a sigh. He's been nothing but kind to both of us since we arrived here... minus the weird wrestling we went through with my first attempt to escape.

His hip undulates again, stealing my attention and pulling me away from my inner thoughts. I whimper. He whines in response and goosebumps pebble my skin. I would never be accepted back in the convent, not after this. I fear their judgment and their condemnation. I was never a perfect sister to begin with and now...

In my conflicted emotions, I push him away and turn, hiding my face. If I can no longer return to my home, where does that leave me? What is my place in this world? The beast crawls and covers my exposed back with his warmth, licking my hair and the shell of my ear. My breath stutters at his persistence.

His hips press against mine and I continue to hide my face. He speaks his language against my ear and my heart races. I wonder what he's saying. It sounds like cooing, like he's trying to calm me.

His claws trail down my side and rips the remnants of my torn habit and I gasp when the cool air hits the back of my thighs. Pressing my legs together, I push back against him to nudge him away but it must get lost in translation because he thrusts right back, a wetness coating my inner thigh again.

This is so wrong.

He mumbles something again and licks. I try to buck him off and hit back with my arms but he catches my wrists and pins it down, a small growl emitting from his throat. It's different from his others, as if laced with words. A few more thrusts and my breast becomes heavy again but with a different feeling. I can feel it leak against the nest and he takes a deep inhale before he lets out a low whine.

I should have put on my undergarments. The fabric had become scratchy with river washing and drying it in the sun. My face flames as his cock slides between my wet folds again and again, asking for entrance.

I'm afraid to give him the answer but I also say nothing, submitting to his quest.

HEMMING

The female smells decadent. Her scent grows muskier as she calls to me with her body. The taste of her milk still on my tongue, my mind is lost in a haze of lust.

My cock strains as it seeks out her hot center, the core scent of her arousal. I'm still wondering whether our kind can mate when my next thrust buries me inside, burning my sensitive flesh. She is like living fire, consuming my soul with her seduction.

She gasps and my body instinctually responds, moving in a rhythm as old as time.

She feels like heaven, I mentally tell myself.

I am only a woman.

My body stiffens and stops. *Did she just...*

Did you just...

You can understand me? Wagging my tail, I wrap my arms around her and pound into her flesh. The decadence of what she freely offers me makes my chest constrict with a hope I never wanted to voice.

She cries into our nest and I begin to worry. *What is it? Have I hurt you? Have I...?*

Don't stop, you beast! Don't tempt me and leave me hanging like this!

Huffing, I snarl and nip at her throat, claiming her with both mind and body. She pants in heat as I give her everything she asks for. Each time her body pushes against mine, my body shudders with pleasure, pounding into her harder and deeper, wanting to unite us as one flesh.

My hairs stand on end as I apply more pressure in my bite. Her rear comes up higher and she plants her face lower into the nest, stretching her neck back further in submission, filling my soul with elation.

I will take care of you little one. Let me be your male. You and the pup will want for nothing.

I-I don't understand...

Let yourself feel. Let me bring you pleasure.

Her mind quiets, obeying my command. Such a beautiful little submissive female—my female. My claws hold her down as my hips continue to invade and conquer. The sound of our combined wetness echoes into the den, filling me with pride. I whine as I bury myself deeply inside of her, my knot enlarging and tying us together as one. Snarling, I hold my growls back for the sake of the still sleeping babe beside us.

She whimpers and I turn her around without removing our connection, licking and sucking at her teats until she calms. Her flesh is soft against my face as I nuzzle and rub my scent all over her chest.

"I can't believe we just did that. This is so wrong."

"How can something that feels so right, be so wrong? You are mine, little female. There is no going back now. You're claimed and mated."

"What are you talking about?" The innocence in her eyes

shines through as she stares at me, making me grin like a thief in the night.

Pressing my muzzle against her neck, I lick the mark I've left behind in our passion. Shoving myself deeper into her, she whimpers again and I wonder if I have done enough to bring her pleasure.

"We shouldn't have done this. Get off me, please!"

Licking her to calm her nerves, I thrust slowly, grinding against her. "It is impossible."

"What do you mean?" she screeches and I cover her mouth with my hand, casting my sight to the side at the pup.

She shakes beneath me, tears running down her face. Why is she sad when I have never felt so invigorated—never felt such purpose in life.

"Calm, female. I will take care of you."

She shoves at my chest and jerks her head to the side until her mouth is free. Her tenacity sends a thrill of excitement through me and I bare my teeth.

"I-I need to think. Get off me." She pulls and tries to roll away only to make me yelp when she tugs at my knot still locked inside of her. "Wha-why are we stuck?"

I huff. "Because, my female. It is how nature intended us to be. Stay with me until I calm you. There is nothing to be afraid of."

Licking her neck, I can feel her silent sobs. I need to make her feel better about us. She is mine now. Licking her teats, I suck. Her endless supply of milk warms my heart, making my hips thrust again.

She quietly moans as I move onto the next breast, my hands caressing her, petting her until her body molds to mine once more.

My tail wags. That's it, pretty female. Let Hemming take care of you. That's a good girl.

H-Hemming? Is that your name?

Remember it, little female for there will be no other male for you. If I even get a sniff of another within a mile of you, I will kill him.

She gasps, her chest sticking out deeper into my mouth as I continue to suck.

I will breed you until you are round with pups, until this den is full of them. Would you like that? Would you like my knot constantly inside of you? Thrusting against her, my knot deflates enough for me to slip out, our combined juices spilling onto the nest, christening it with our mating scent.

I moan at the smell, still lost in the aftereffects of lust as I crawl down her body and push her legs apart for better access.

"What are you doing?"

I answer her with my tongue deep inside of her delicious pussy, lapping up everything she has to offer me. How can a single female taste so sweet all over?

She tries to close her legs around my head and I growl in warning until she submits and opens her legs wider. She bites her bottom lip in worry and my heart swells. She must learn to trust her mate. I will keep her safe.

I will keep her happy.

Nipping at her tender flesh, my cock hardens again, making me groan. There is a nub at the top of her pussy, hooded and hiding. My curiosity getting the better of me, I suck on it like I did her breast and her hips undulate. My tail wagging harder, I continue to tease until her body is strung tight like a hunter's bow. How very curious. Nipping it, her little fingers grab the back of my head and grip my fur. My hackles rising to what feels like an unknown threat, I suck and bite, lick and play until she cries out in pleasure, deafening my ears and waking the pup.

He wails and she whimpers. My cock leaks in response but I

let her tend to the pup when she attempts to roll over toward him.

On my elbows and knees, I watch with my ears flicked back. She cradles him to her chest, offering him what I was tasting earlier and I find myself pricked with jealousy. Does he taste how sweet she is? How warm her milk flows into his mouth. Does he feel how her soul pours out with love? I greedily want all her love and I chastise myself for envying a pup of all things.

Shaking my head, my ears straighten and I'm clouded in shame for feeling this way. What is wrong with me? Leaping out of the nest, I quickly exit the den and let myself run through the woods—run until my limbs scream at me with ache.

The moon stares down at me in accusation as I leap onto boulders and growl at myself. I howl in confusion and tackle anything that stands in my way. Something shifts ahead of me, the sound of rustling leaves attracting my attention. My mind focuses on the hunt as I trail behind the creature quickly between the trees.

I hit a clearing, the moon shining down on my black fur. Howling with my nose in the air, I catch the scent of my prey once more. Darting between trees and leaping over uneven terrain, I cut off the creature and take it down with a bite to the neck and its warm blood flowing between my fangs.

The tangy taste of copper that usually satisfies my hunger when I'm worked up like this, only makes me miss the warmth of my female. Shaking myself, I drag the deer back towards the den in hopes of asking her for forgiveness.

Nine

JEANNA

I'm at a loss at why he left so abruptly the way he did.

Hemming...

His name in my mind warms me in strange ways. My cheeks flame at the thought of him inside of me, at the thought of his mouth on me in ways he shouldn't have but did anyway.

I should be scared. I should be appalled at everything that's happened. Instead, I'm worried about him. Is he alright? Was he mad?

Baby Adam hiccups as he releases my nipple and falls back into a milk coma.

Hemming. I never even got a chance to tell him my name.

I am here, my female. Do not worry so. I can feel your emotions through our link.

Link? What is he talking about? Does it have to do with the fact that I can understand a beast in my mind? I must really be going crazy being away from society this long.

I can physically hear him huff in laughter even though I cannot see him. I smile in response even if he can't see me.

I can feel you. I am glad you were thinking of me.

A rustle makes me startle and jump only to find Hemming dragging back a deer into the den. His eyes flick to the baby and then to me. *I've taken this kill down for you, my female.*

"Jeanna."

Jeanna. A name worthy of such beauty. He lays the dead deer beside the nest and keeps his body down beside it. I am so confused.

"What are you doing?"

I've come back to apologize.

Suddenly, different worries overtake me. I never thought I would be rejected by a beast. My mood tanks.

He quickly stands up and pounces on me, taking me to my back as he rubs his face all over my chin, cheek and chest.

Do not feel this way, my Jeanna. I came to apologize for being jealous of your pup. I was lost in you. Seeing you care for the pup made me greedy for you to care for me the same way. I wanted your attention, I wanted your love. It is not my place to demand such things when there is a defenseless babe that requires more from you.

What does one say to that? He's filled my heart back with warmth as he continues to rub his body on me, tickling my skin.

Tentatively, I wrap my arms around him, wanting to comfort him as well. We stay that way for a short time until I'm reminded that I need to tend to the deer before it starts to smell.

Rest, my Jeanna. I shall provide for you and burn the meat to your satisfaction.

A laugh escapes me. "Burn the meat?"

It is what you enjoy, no? I have watched you. You humans have strange customs.

I bury my face against his fur and laugh earnestly. He huffs against me and lets out a low rumble, one that calms my soul.

"Hemming."

He shoves his nose against my face and licks me.

"Why do you live alone in this cave?" My other question lingers in my mind: do you not have family? Do you not have a pack?

He mentally sighs and rests his head against my shoulder, staring at baby Adam. *I had a pack. I am cursed with my sire's size and temper. The pack grew to fear me—an alpha with fur as black as death. I became known as a death dealer, one they could not trust during the hunt. I isolated myself. I didn't want to put any of them or their pups in danger.*

Grabbing his face between my hands, I bring him up to face me, trying to see what he's telling me.

"I do not believe it. I've seen you, been with you. You are not what they say you are."

You do not know this.

"How can someone in awareness of danger enough to remove themselves actually be such a threat?"

He stands up on all fours above me, removing my hands from his face. Leaning in, he stares at me with intensity. *Do not forget how I found you, my little Jeanna. I slaughtered your people.*

My heart skips a beat at his statement. But hope takes over. "But you spared me and baby Adam."

His lips curl into a snarl right before he leaves me and drags the deer to the other side of the room with his mouth. I sit up, watching him work in silence. There's an internal battle going on here, one that I'm not privy to despite our newly established link.

I project the image of me holding him and his back tenses, his hairs stand up, and his ears flick back against his head.

A few minutes in, his tail slowly wags and I let out a sigh. It seems we're both plagued with our own inner turmoil. Leaving him be, I lay back down, turn over and pull baby Adam into my arms.

My mind drifts in and out of sleep. Images of bloodshed, my mother's screams, the baby's screams and finally fur as black as midnight. Warmth envelopes me as a furred arm comes around and pulls us both closer together.

The combined body heat irritates the baby, making him kick away from us. I smile, turning around and wrapping my arms around a beast that's informed me he's known nothing but rejection from the people who should have been family. Rubbing my own face against his chest, I listen to his heart beat.

We are kindred spirits, you and I. The Lord has brought us together for a reason.

What do you mean?

Lifting my head, I place my chin on his chest. His head is too tall above me as we lay on our sides, so I stare at the column of his throat as I continue my thoughts.

You can say, I understand. My father had... rejected my mother and I. We found sanctuary in a different home but even then it was not a smooth transition. I was never the perfect sister for the convent, my past haunting me from time to time.

Running my fingers through his fur, I trace his skin until I reach his jaw.

I thought I was broken. I thought the Lord couldn't use me anymore. But baby Adam changed that. I had a new purpose. I had someone to protect.

He tips his face down and stares at me. *You scented of fear and my protective instincts took over. You and the pup were the only things I could see in my anger and fury.*

Something comes over me, as if this moment is monumental. Looking over my shoulder, I make sure the baby is still asleep before I climb over Hemming and straddle him. I can hear his tail wag, rustling against the leaves and moss of our nest and it makes me smile.

He was right about one thing. How can something that feels so right, be so wrong? If the Lord knows all his plans for us, did he not also know that this would happen? That I would find myself enamored with Hemming, that I would find myself whole with him.

Two broken souls brought together. Were we left to wander our own battlefields just so that our meeting would come to be?

His hips thrust up with his hard cock again. Unashamedly, my legs open wider and slip him in. My pussy stretches around his girth at this angle, making me whimper. His arms come around me and he rumbles against my chest, relaxing me enough to take him in further.

You burn me, sear my soul with your heat. I'm lost in everything that is my female.

My face flushes at his words while he stretches me again and again with every thrust. I feel full, I feel whole.

Listening to him pant against me, my breasts become heavy with milk, making me moan. As if reading my thoughts, he shifts me off his cock and shoves my right breast into his mouth, pulling mouthfuls of milk. I sigh as he moves to the left, then grabs my hips and shoves me back on his angry red cock that's glistening between us with one hard push.

I'm dazed with all the sensations I'm trying to process. He flips us over and begins to pound me while clamping his jaws around my shoulder, licking it. He's so primal that I can feel my pussy flutter in response to his dominance.

He mentally groans and my pussy clamps down. *I love the way you submit to me, my female. It makes me want to bury my cock so deeply inside of you that you won't be able to move for days.*

"Hemming!"

He growls at the sound of his name, pushing the back of my

legs up and thrusting delicious friction between my legs. He grunts at the crook of my neck as his body tenses up right before he buries himself deep inside, expanding inside of me.

Licking my face, he grabs my hand and shoves it between us. *I want to watch you bring pleasure to yourself.* He forces my finger on my clit and I shyly look away. I *want to watch my Jeanna come undone around my cock inside of her.*

I shake my head and he growls against my ear. *Your male demands it. I want to feel you squeeze my knot, knowing you belong to me.*

Biting my bottom lip, my fingers begin to slowly play. Still sensitive from our activity and the fact that we're locked together, pleasure rises quickly with each stroke and each pinch.

Hemming licks my neck and his mark on my shoulder, nipping at it lovingly as my muscles tighten more and more until I push myself over the cliff and moan.

That's a good female, he groans mentally. *I love the way you milk me.*

HEMMING

The babe grows quickly, stumbling around the grass as he tries to walk on his hind legs. I watch with mirth as he laughs only the way babies do when they find joy in life. It will be good to give him brothers and sisters.

Standing vigil, I sneak glances at my female as she bathes herself in the river, her dark hair gleaming in the sun. She is the most beautiful thing I've ever seen.

My nose catches a scent in the air and my hairs stand.

Jeanna, grab the pup and go back to the den.

Her head snaps to mine with concern right before she does exactly as I have instructed. The pup squeals when she picks him up and my ears flick back. Leaping down from the rock I'm perched on, I sniff the air again.

Humans. Males. Full of leathers.

Hunters.

Making sure my pack reaches safety, I kick more bushes towards the entrance and double back around to find the source of the threat.

I spot three humans with rifles walking through the woods not far from our home. Growling, they jump and look around them, unable to locate the sound. Hiding behind the trees, I slink around, casting rocks to the side, separating one of the men.

"I'll go check that out. Watch my back."

"If it's a big one, make sure you bag it in one piece. Pelts bring in a mint."

"I ain't that sloppy of a shot, you asshole."

"Yeah, yeah. Whatever."

Once he's far enough from the group, I pounce, twisting his neck easily. He falls to the ground and I investigate his coverings. Knives, more guns.

"What the hell is taking him so long?"

"Just leave him. He was a worthless piece of shit anyway."

The lack of loyalty makes me lift my lip in a snarl. I watch as they walk the opposite direction of the den and return home through the back entrance.

"Hemming?"

Yes, my mate. I have returned.

"Is everything okay?"

I crawl into our nest beside her and lick her face in reassurance. When she tires of my antics, she pushes me away and rolls her eyes. The pup tries to follow her and I pounce on him, making him squeal with laughter.

My mate walks around gathering the wood I've accumulated inside to start on dinner. Tickling the pup's tummy with my nose, my ears flick forward when a twig snaps outside.

Gently dropping him into the nest, I get on all fours and creep toward the entrance of the cave. The barrel of a gun hits me in the nose as I growl and walk backward.

My female gasps behind me and my hairs stand at attention.

Protect the pup and yourself. If anything happens, just leave me.

What? What are you talking about? Why are you saying this?

I growl when the single stranger lifts his head to look over my shoulder. He smells of bad spirits and evil intent. They always do.

"Well, lookie here," he announces as he smiles with menace. "Is this where you've been hiding, Jeanna? Where is that whore of a mother of yours?"

I slap his gun and leap. The stranger twists his weapon and slams my face with the butt of his gun, dazing me.

"Get off me! Let him go!"

I shake my head and swipe at the stranger's back only to rip off his bag. My mate screams when he tosses her down and I see red. A new emotion I've never experienced overtakes me. My fists and claws work on their own accord, my maw crunches down on bone and shakes until the flesh in my mouth explodes with blood.

"Ahhh! You fucking beast! I'll kill you!"

Lost in my bites and bloodlust, I don't see the ax he pulls out and swings over his head.

"No!" my mate cries, right before she tackles him and takes us all down to the ground.

"You good for nothing whore!" He elbows her, throwing her off him.

"You vile human!" I snarl right before I clamp down on his offending limb, biting, crunching and ripping it off. Everything becomes tunnel vision as I stare at his slack mouth and smell his fear. Opening my maw, I smell nothing but the copper of his lifeforce. Biting down on his neck, satisfaction courses through me at the sound of his gurgling.

"What the hell? What is a woman doing here? Are you a

monster fucker?" The second male's voice drifts and I stand on my hind legs with the dead male still in my mouth. Releasing him, I toss his body against the remaining stranger and attack without remorse.

They dare enter my home and threaten my pack? Death will be the only thing they find here.

I listen to his screams as I tear apart his legs and claw at his face, my fingers slipping through the blood.

When the haze finally dies down, I turn to find a familiar sight. My female crouched down with the babe at her breast. Her eyes are locked on the bodies littered at my feet. Taking tentative steps towards her, her focus shoots to me and what I find there fills me with guilt and remorse.

Fear.

A new rage brews within me—not at my family but myself. How could I have let myself get so lost in the bloodlust? Will her view of me forever be tainted by this? The others were right all along. I am nothing but a death dealer.

Confusion and self hatred coursing through me, I howl in pain and turn to leave the den. The blood in my mouth makes my tongue loll out, licking away the remnants of my enemies. I leap against trees and boulders, pushing my muscles to their limits as the sun begins to go down in the sky. Lost on a run to escape the skeletons of my past, I let myself feel every burn and every ache.

My instincts led me home without intending to come back. I skid to a halt on the ground, panting and lifting my head to the moon that now looks down on me with accusation. It is also tinged with red, a reminder of all that my life has in store for me: death and destruction.

Hemming, please. Please if you can hear me, come back to me. We need you. I need you.

My ears flick back and forth, uncertain whether this is a farce. How can my mate still need a killer? A murderer?

Please, Hemming! Lord give me strength. I cannot make it on my own. I need my mate.

Her mental cries of anguish prick my heart with more pain than my body could ever experience. Shaking my fur, I roll my shoulders and humble myself, crawling back into our den cautiously.

She cries out, startled, when the leaves crunch at my entrance. She then surprises me by leaving the babe in the nest and running into my arms, wrapping hers around me so tightly in an embrace that I lose breath.

Hemming! I was so worried about you. Don't ever do that again!

I couldn't face you. I couldn't stand the smell of your fear.

She cradles my face and presses her forehead to mine. It breaks my heart to know that she will no longer love the beast that I am.

"How can you say that? You protected us. You saved us. My father would have never let me leave here alive, let alone the baby."

My fury is unpredictable. You do not deserve a mate who has nothing but death as a companion.

"You silly beast! I don't want anyone else but you!"

How can you still want a monster? One that's still covered in the blood of his enemies.

"Because you loved me first. You cared for us when nothing made any sense. And love conquers all, Hemming. Never forget that. We'll get through this. I need you to trust me—to trust my devotion to our family."

I stare at her then, really stare at her. Her wet eyes glisten as tears stream down her face. This brave creature before me scares me. That was the new emotion I couldn't identify earlier. I thought I was going to lose her, if not by bloodshed then by everything I've made her witness.

What if it happens again and I cannot control the rage?

She kisses my nose and closes her eyes making more tears escape the corner of her eyes. "Then we have faith, Hemming. I have faith in you."

And like that, my hardened heart shatters into a million pieces, all for this little, brave female before me. Bringing myself toward the ground on all fours, I tilt my head and expose my neck to her, submitting to her strength.

The babe waddles over and lands on me, gripping my dark fur in an embrace. I whine at whatever higher power my female always prays to with eternal gratitude for bringing them into my life.

Epilogue

JEANNA

I needed new clothes or else I would have never taken this trip. Hemming tries his best to give us what we need, but his knowledge of female coverings is very limited.

Hemming sneezes behind me the closer we get to town and I shush him with my finger to my lips.

It is not my fault there are so many scents in one location. Why do you humans have to mix so many smells together all the time?

Can you just keep it together over there quietly? What is the baby doing? Make sure he stays out of trouble.

He is biting my tail. He's doing fine. I will keep an eye on him. Just hurry, my mate. Our distance is making me agitated.

Hold your horses. This has to be done strategically.

I told you I could steal whatever you need.

Yeah, and you'll cause hysteria at the same time. No, thank you. Oh!

Someone walks by with a basket of vegetables and I jump at the opportunity. Clearing my throat, I rub down the torn habit dress I have on. Hopefully the stranger will not recognize it as such since the dark fabric has been worn down.

"Excuse me. I was wondering if you had an extra set of clothes you could spare me? I seem to have gotten into some trouble."

She looks at me from head to toe curiously. "Where did you come from? Out there? Don't you know there are beasts that roam the land?"

I smile weakly, not wanting to give anything away.

She leans in and whispers, "I hear the howling at night. The tales say a beast as black as death lurks around these parts, devouring wandering humans. You best be careful, love. Come, I have a spare dress out on the line right now."

"Thank you so very much."

Don't go too far, female. I do not trust her. I will follow right behind you.

Hemming! Stay out of sight.

The stranger leads me to a small home on the outskirts of town. Thank goodness. I watch her put down her basket and reach for the clothes pins, handing me the dress.

"There you go, that should fit. We look about the same size."

I quickly take off my dress and put hers on. She gasps and my eyes shoot to hers.

"My dear, you are with child! Would you like me to take you to the convent? They may be able to help you in your condition."

My chest constricts for a second with longing for a life I left behind, but then warms with thoughts of my beloved mate waiting for my return with our baby.

"I thank you for your offer, kind miss. But a dress is all I need." With a soft smile, I grab the remnants of my habit, turn, and make my way back into the woods.

I barely make it to our meeting spot when a little body tackles me and hugs my leg. Another large, furred body embraces me from behind, sniffing my skin and new clothes.

I don't like the way it smells. It doesn't smell like you.

"Well, you're going to have to get used to it because you've practically destroyed the other dress."

He rears back, his ears flattening on his head. *I can steal you a million dresses if you would just forgive me.*

Turning in his arms, I pull his head down toward me. "Faith, hope and love. But the greatest of these is love. Hemming, a dress can be replaced. You, my beloved mate, can not. I will always forgive you."

I don't deserve you.

"But I love you anyway."

His ears straighten and his tongue lolls out in joy right before he lifts his head and howls.

About the Author

If you get your kicks in a magical manner, order toys from websites like bad dragon, and prefer your monsters *in* your bed instead of *under* them, then Y. D. is your girl.

Writing everything from spicy dark fantasy to fluffier-than-a-cool-marshmallow romance, Y.D. La Mar has her fingers in all sorts of man-meat pie, and the sky is the limit. Somehow, this magical mistress manages to balance her spicy author life with her responsibilities as a mom, a wife, and a resident of Sin City —*oh, irony, you've felled me.*

When the world is full of black-and-white, Y.D. plays in the grey zones, spending her time creating new ways to shock and awe her editor, as well as her readers.

Follow Me!

FLOWCODE
PRIVACY.FLOWCODE.COM

Also by Y.D. La Mar

STREET ARRHYTHMIA TRILOGY

The Scent of Jasmine

For The Love of Import & Blood

To The Beat of The Streets

Spinoff

Arachnophilia

REVERSE HAREM

Warring Suns

SCI FI

The Essence of Esme

PARANORMAL

The Hunger of Thieves

Heart of The Reaper

Heart of the Reaper: Tales from the Underworld

Soul of The Reaper

Fate of The Reaper

Bury Me Alive

Lead Me Through The Fire

PSYCHOLOGICAL THRILLER

The Truth Enslaved

CONTEMPORARY

The Formation of Us

The Conception of Us

The Revelation of Us

The House of Eden (cowrite)

When the Bloom Burns (cowrite)

OMEGAVERSE

Gero

Bernhard

Severin

DYSTOPIAN/POST APOCALYPTIC

We Are the Fallen

MONSTER SHORT STORIES

Sinful Attraction

The Sky Below

Maeonia

Between Heaven and Earth

Fantasies Inflamed

Her 13th Hour

Ignus Fatuus

ANTHOLOGIES

Used and Bound

Captured by Darkness

Until the End

After the Rain

Into The Woods

A Foster Fling

Bound by Monsters

Once Upon a Nightmare

Monsters in Love: Lost in the Dark

Monsters in Love: Lost in the Forest

Monsters in Love: Monstrous Ever After

Monsters in Love: Lost in the Deeps

Monsters in Love: Aloha Nui Loa

Pollinators

The Red Key Club: Valentines Day Edition

The Red Key Club: Halloween Edition

Creepy Court

Crimson Vendetta

For the Love of Villains

SHARED WORLDS

Inferno World

Games of the Underworld

Rise of the Dreads

Monsters Ball

Rescue Me: A Hero Romance Collection